Pigs Might Fly!

The Further Adventures of
the Three Little Pigs

Jonathan Emmett & Steve Cox

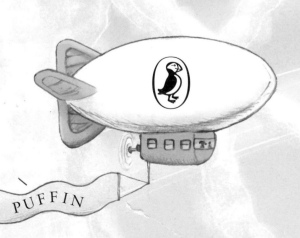

PUFFIN

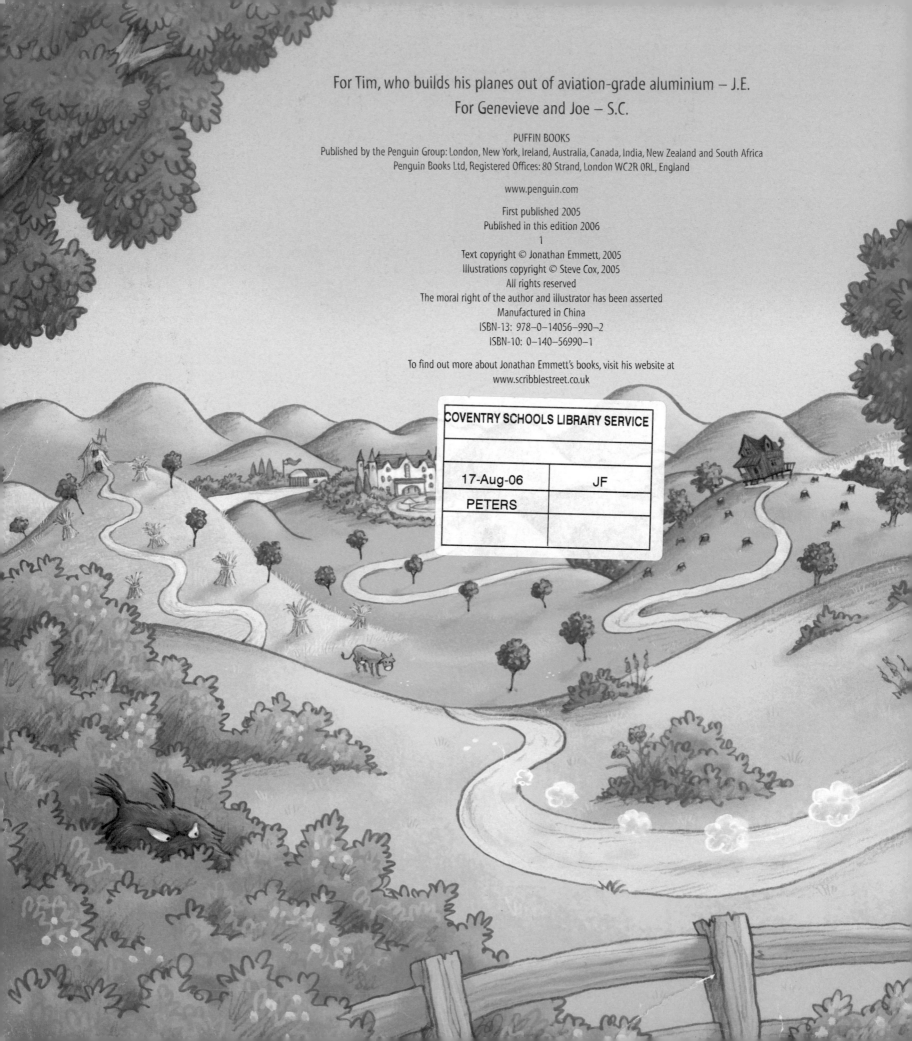

For Tim, who builds his planes out of aviation-grade aluminium – J.E.
For Genevieve and Joe – S.C.

PUFFIN BOOKS
Published by the Penguin Group: London, New York, Ireland, Australia, Canada, India, New Zealand and South Africa
Penguin Books Ltd, Registered Offices: 80 Strand, London WC2R 0RL, England

www.penguin.com

First published 2005
Published in this edition 2006
1
Text copyright © Jonathan Emmett, 2005
Illustrations copyright © Steve Cox, 2005
All rights reserved
The moral right of the author and illustrator has been asserted
Manufactured in China
ISBN-13: 978–0–14056–990–2
ISBN-10: 0–140–56990–1

To find out more about Jonathan Emmett's books, visit his website at
www.scribblestreet.co.uk

COVENTRY SCHOOLS LIBRARY SERVICE

| 17-Aug-06 | JF |
| PETERS | |

Once upon a time there were three little pigs,
but I'm sure you know that story already.
This is the story of what happened next, SO . . .

Twice upon a time there were
three not-so-little pigs.
Their names were . . .

Woody,

Waldo

and
Wilbur.

This is **Waldo**.

Waldo was **not** the **cleverest** of pigs, and he **never** learnt by his mistakes. After his straw house, he had tried to build a straw television and **even** a straw bicycle.

This is **Woody**.

Woody was cleverer than **Waldo**, but he **wasn't** very **careful**. So, while the things that **Woody** built often looked impressive . . .

. . . they **didn't** last for **very** long!

And this is Wilbur.

Wilbur was the smart pig of the litter.
When Wilbur built something,
he always went the
whole hog
and built
it properly.

Oh yes – and this is the
BIG BAD WOLF
(whose real name was Algernon,
so you can see why he never
told anybody).

WHAT A PORKER!

WOLF IS FOXED

3 PIGS SAVE THEIR OWN BACON

TAIL-END CHARLIE

BUM-BOILED PLOT!

GLUE

HUFF AND NONSENSE

BOTTOM OINKMENT

HAM-FISTED ATTEMPT

ALGERNON IS A BIG WUSS SAYS PIG

The **WOLF** was still sore
about what had happened the first
time he'd climbed down the three pigs' chimney.
In fact, his bottom was SO badly scalded,
he still couldn't sit down properly!

One day
Wilbur saw this advert
in his newspaper.

"That sounds like a prize worth **winning**,"
thought **Wilbur**, licking his lips.
When **Waldo** and **Woody** heard about the race, they
were just as keen to enter. And so each pig set about
building an aeroplane.

Waldo thought that he should
stick to what he knew best.

So he built his plane out of
– can you guess?

Yes, **STRAW!**

Woody usually threw things together from whatever was lying around.

So he built his plane out of — can you guess?

Yes, **STICKS!**

And **Wilbur**? Well, at first **Wilbur** didn't build anything. He just drew **lots** of pictures.

Wilbur was still drawing when **Waldo** and **Woody** had finished building their planes. "I want to make sure that **everything** works **properly**," he explained.

When **Wilbur** finally started,
he built his plane out of – can you guess?
NO, not **bricks** – whoever heard of an aeroplane
made out of **bricks**? He built it out of
metal, of course.

All this time the
BIG BAD WOLF
had been spying on the pigs ...

"At last," he grinned,
"my chance for **revenge!**"
"I'll stop those pigs from **hogging** all the
glory," he thought. "I'll **win** that air race.
Then I'll **wolf** down those pies and have
those three **porkers** for pudding!"

On the day of the race all the aeroplanes
were lined up and ready to go.

The BIG BAD
WOLF

had brought along his own plane
and was wearing a sheepskin
flying jacket and hat as a disguise . . .

PATTERSON'S

AIR RACE TODAY

He sneaked round the back
of **Wilbur's** jet and
drained out **all** the fuel.

A horn sounded and the race began!

Waldo's aeroplane **wobbled** down the runway ...

Woody's aeroplane **rattled** down the runway ...

BUT ... **Wilbur's** aeroplane **didn't** move at all!

Waldo's straw aeroplane had only made it halfway down the runway when the **WOLF** came speeding up behind him.

"LET ME WIN, LITTLE PIG, LET ME WIN!" he shouted.

"Not by the hair on my chinny chin chin!" called Waldo.

Woody's aeroplane had started well, but it began to fall apart in the air. The wolf came whizzing up.

"LET ME WIN, LITTLE PIG, LET ME WIN!"

he shouted.

"Not by the hair on my chinny chin chin!" called Woody.

"Then I'll **VROOM**

and I'll **ZOOM**

and I'll **SMASH** your plane in!" cried the wolf.

And he drove his jet – **CRASH** – right through

the middle of **Woody's** aeroplane and smashed it to pieces!

The wolf was now SO sure
he was going to WIN the race,
that he decided to show off a bit.

**"LOOK AT ME!
LOOK AT ME!"** he cried.

And he *looped* the *loop*.

He had just finished his daring display   when...

"WHEEEEEE!"

...who should come flying past, but

the three pigs!

the three pigs!

Wilbur had refuelled his jet and picked up the others.

Now **they** were ahead of the **wolf!**

The **WOLF** was furious!

"LET ME WIN,
LITTLE PIGS,
LET ME
WIN!"
shouted the wolf.

"Not by the hair on our chinny chin chins!" called all the pigs.

"Then I'll **VROOM** and I'll **ZOOM** and I'll **SMASH** your plane in!" cried the wolf.

But, try as he might, the wolf could NOT bring down Wilbur's aeroplane!

"Right," thought the **WOLF**, "if that
plane is going to win, then I'm
going to be the one flying it."

So he
jumped
out
of his plane . . .

. . . and landed behind the huge
barrel at the back of Wilbur's jet.

"What is this thing anyway?" he wondered.
"It looks like a big metal CHIMNEY,"
he thought, sticking his
head inside . . .

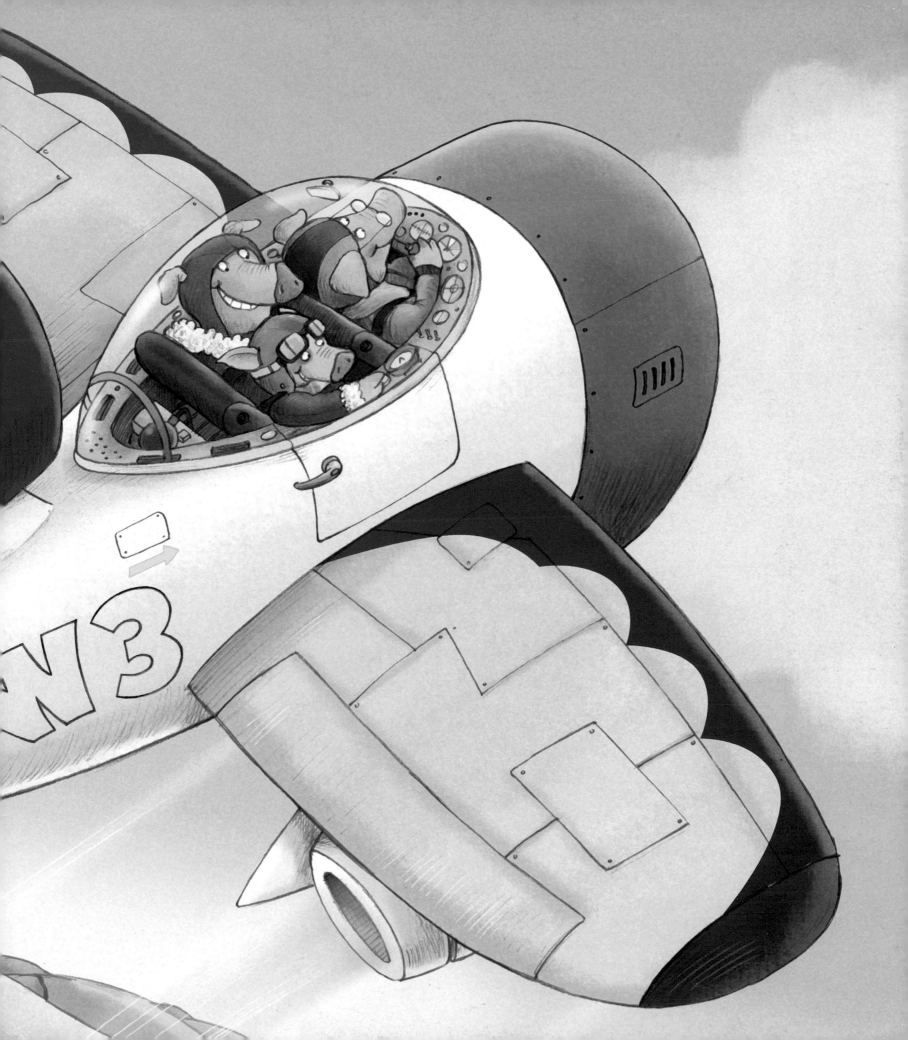

Waldo and Woody had
also noticed the huge metal barrel.
"What is that thing anyway?"
asked Waldo.

"It's a **rocket booster**," explained Wilbur.

"What does it do?" asked **Woody**.

"**THIS!**" said Wilbur, pushing a **big** red button.

3 8002 01416 5940

A huge flame **shot** out of the rocket booster,
the wolf **blasted** backwards . . .
and the jet **whooshed** forward . . .
. . . OVER THE FINISHING LINE!

"We did it!" cheered the pigs. "We won!"

"What happened to that other pilot?" asked **Waldo**.

"I bet he didn't want to **hang around**," said **Woody**.

"Yes," grinned **Wilbur**, "I expect he's a
sore loser. A **very sore** loser indeed!"